Sidney & Sydney
BOOK 3

Big Dog Decisions

by Michele Jakubowski ★ illustrated by Luisa Montalto

PICTURE WINDOW BOOKS
a capstone imprint

Sidney & Sydney is published by Picture Window Books
A Capstone Imprint
1710 Roe Crest Drive
North Mankato, Minnesota 56003
www.capstoneyoungreaders.com

Library of Congress Cataloging-in-Publication Data
Jakubowski, Michele, author.
Big dog decisions / by Michele Jakubowski ; illustrated by Luisa Montalto.
pages cm. -- (Sidney & Sydney ; [bk. 3])
Summary: Sidney's mother refuses to let him have a dog, so when his friend
Sydney comes up with the idea of starting a dog-walking business, it seems
like a way to have dogs to play with and make money at the same time – but
soon the friends find out that dogs are a lot of work, and can really strain a
friendship.
ISBN 978-1-4795-5226-9 (hardcover)
ISBN 978-1-4795-5227-6 (paper over board)
1. Dog walking--Juvenile fiction. 2. Dogs--Juvenile fiction. 3. Friendship--
Juvenile fiction. 4. Money-making projects for children--Juvenile fiction.
5. Responsibility--Juvenile fiction. [1. Dog walking--Fiction. 2. Dogs--Fiction.
3. Friendship--Fiction. 4. Moneymaking projects--Fiction. 5. Responsibility--
Fiction.] I. Montalto, Luisa, illustrator. II. Title.
PZ7.J153555Bi 2014

813.6--dc23   2013047091

Design: Kristi Carlson

Printed in China.
032014
008116WAIF14

FOR GINGER, THE GREATEST DOG
IN THE WORLD.
—M.J.

TABLE OF CONTENTS

Name: Sydney Shelby Baxter Greene
Age: 8
Birthdate: August 3
Parents: Bob and Jane Greene
Siblings: Owen (my baby brother)
Hobbies: fashion, playing *Galaxy Conquest*, reading

Harley and Sydney — best friends

Sydney Greene

is a sassy third grader. Not only does she love fashion, but she loves a good game of *Galaxy Conquest* as well. She might be the smallest kid in the class, but she's also the spunkiest! Her best friend is Harley Livingston, a third-grade soccer star. They have been best friends since preschool, when Harley kicked a soccer ball into Sydney's face.

Name: Sidney Patrick Fletcher
Age: 8
Birthdate: May 11
Parents: Paula Fletcher
Siblings: None
Hobbies: sports, playing *Galaxy Conquest*, telling jokes

Sidney and best friend Gomez

Sidney Fletcher

is a quiet kid who loves sports. He is also the newest third grader in Oak Grove. However, it didn't take him long to make friends. Gomez (whose real name is Marco Xavier Gomez) is Sidney's first and best friend in Oak Grove. With one joke at the bus stop, Sidney and Gomez became inseparable.

CHAPTER 1

I Want a Crazy Dog

I've never had a pet. We used to live in an apartment in Chicago. It was too small for a pet. Or at least that's what my mom told me. I didn't think it was too small for a fish, but my mom said the no pet rule covered every kind of pet — even fish.

We moved from Chicago to Oak Grove after my dad died. Even though we live in a house with a big yard, we still don't have any pets. It doesn't seem fair.

My friend Nathan has a new puppy. I'm pretty sure everyone in the world has a puppy but me. Well, me and my best friend, Gomez. Me and Gomez were going to Nathan's house to see his new puppy. I already felt jealous, and we hadn't even seen the dog yet.

Before we even made it into the yard, a small puppy jumped on Gomez. Gomez was not a big kid, and the puppy knocked him right over.

"Get him off me!" Gomez shouted.

"Calm down, Gomez," Nathan said as he pulled the puppy off of him. I couldn't help laughing at Gomez. Who else gets knocked over by a tiny puppy?

"His name is Calvin. I got to name him," Nathan said with a big smile.

"I wanted to name him Hershey," Nathan's little sister Natalie said.

"You got to name him by yourself?" I asked. That was so cool! Beside my stuffed bear Ted I'd never named anything.

"He's a Labrador retriever," Nathan told us. "Since he's brown, he's actually called a chocolate lab. He's only six weeks old. When he grows up he'll be over sixty pounds."

Instead of thinking about sixty pounds of chocolate like I normally would, I thought about how much I wanted a dog. Nathan's dog was crazy! He had been running and jumping since we'd gotten to Nathan's house. I wanted a crazy dog, too!

"He sleeps on the floor in my room. I get to walk him every day and get his food and water. I even get to give him his bath!" Nathan said.

"You are so lucky," I told Nathan.

"You sure are," Gomez agreed. "I wish we could stay and play with Calvin, but we have to get home for dinner."

* * *

The whole way home from Nathan's house I thought about getting a dog. It would be so much fun.

"I'd name him Sidney, Jr.," I told Gomez.

"Oh no!" Gomez said. "There are already enough people with that name in Oak Grove!"

Gomez and I are friends with a girl named Sydney. When I moved to Oak Grove there was a lot of confusion because we both have the same name. Our names aren't spelled the same, but it's still a little confusing. Now we laugh about the situation. She's pretty cool for a girl. So is her best friend, Harley.

"That's true," I said. "Maybe I'd name my dog Payton after Walter Payton. He was an amazing Chicago Bears football player and my dad's all-time favorite. My dog Payton would be fast like a football player, and I'd teach him how to play catch." The more I thought about it, the more I wanted a dog. In fact, I needed a dog!

"I'd get one of those long dogs that looks like a hot dog. I'd name him Oscar," Gomez said. "Get it?"

"That is funny! Payton and Oscar would be best friends — just like us!" I said, getting excited.

The more we talked about it, the more I realized how much I needed a dog. My life depended on it! (I guess that's a little dramatic, but I needed to get my point across.) Now I just needed to figure out how to convince my mom.

CHAPTER 2

Puppy in a Purse

"Got you!" I shouted as I blasted Sidney with a turbo double-strike laser. We were playing *Galaxy Conquest 2*, and I had beaten him two games in a row. This was unusual, because Sidney likes to win as much as I do, and he is a very good *Galaxy Conquest 2* player.

"Yeah, yeah," he said. "I'd also teach Payton how to fetch my shoes in the morning. Then I'd never have to look for them. Payton would do all the work for me. Wouldn't that be so great?"

At first I only hung out with Sidney out of convenience because our moms are best friends and hang out all the time. But now I actually consider him one of my good friends. I usually like playing video games with him. However, today he was being really annoying. He wouldn't stop talking about getting a stupid dog!

"Why don't you just put your shoes by the door? Then you'd never lose them. Then you don't need a dog," I suggested. I love fashion and wouldn't dream of losing a pair of my cute shoes.

"What?" Sidney looked confused. "It's not about losing my shoes. I just really want a dog!"

"I know! You've been talking about it nonstop since you got here." I set the controller down. What was the point of beating him in a game when he wasn't really trying?

"I thought you wanted one of those little dogs," Sidney said.

"I used to, but I haven't thought about it in a long time," I said.

"How come?" he asked.

"I almost got one, but then my mom found out she was going to have a baby. Once Owen was born, she said she couldn't take care of a new baby and a puppy," I told him.

"That's too bad," Sidney said.

Thinking about carrying around a little puppy in a purse made me remember how much I'd wanted one. Owen was cute, but he was not the same thing as a puppy.

Sidney had a little smile on his face. "How old is Owen now?"

"He'll be two on his next birthday," I said.

"And when was the last time you asked your parents about getting a dog?" he asked.

At first I couldn't remember. It had been a long time. "I guess it was before Owen was born."

Sidney smiled even bigger. "Maybe it's been long enough. Owen is getting older and a little easier to deal with. Maybe they'll say yes now. We should both ask our parents at dinner tonight."

"That's a great idea! They have a hard time saying no when we both ask!"

"Yeah, the two of us can talk them in to anything," Sidney said. "Let's do it!"

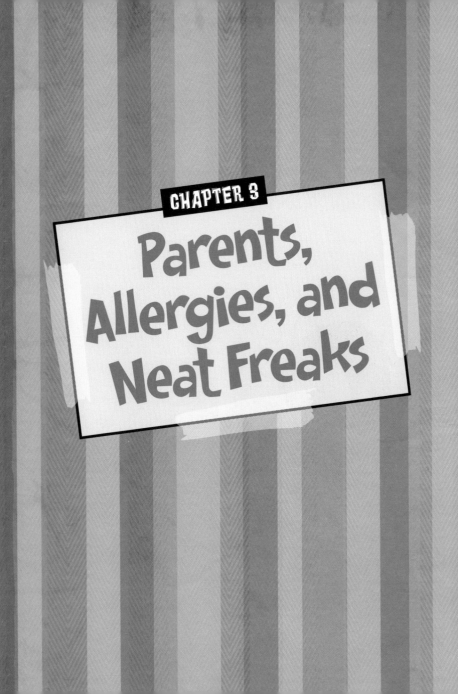

CHAPTER 3

Parents, Allergies, and Neat Freaks

"I can't believe they said no," Sydney said sadly.

It was the day after we had the big dog discussion. Sydney and I were sitting out in front of my house with Gomez and Harley. We had both been in bad moods all day. We both really wanted a dog.

At first it had looked like our parents might say yes. We had planned it perfectly. We waited until everyone had finished eating. The adults were sitting around the table talking and laughing. Sydney's dad had just told a story about some funny thing that happened at work. Both of our moms were cracking up.

I looked at Sydney and nodded my head. It was go time. I told them about Nathan's new puppy. Then we both asked nicely if we could get dogs. We even remembered to say please.

At first our parents didn't say anything. I thought that was a good sign. Then they all started talking at once about how much work a dog was and what a big responsibility it was. They said it costs a lot of money to take care of a dog.

Sydney and I looked at each other across the table. We knew the answer was no. Sydney's parents and my mom agreed that neither of us was ready to have a dog. I was sad and mad and annoyed.

I had to complain to my friends. "I am so ready to have a dog! I'm very responsible. I remember to brush my teeth every night without my mom having to tell me. Well, at least most nights."

"I'm responsible, too, and I'll never get a dog," Gomez said. "My sister Sophia is so allergic that she sneezes when she even thinks about a dog."

"I'll never get a dog either." Harley frowned. "My mom is such a neat freak.

She would go nuts if a single piece of fur landed on her floor."

"When I grow up, I'm going to have a whole bunch of dogs," I said.

"Me too!" said Gomez. "Too bad that's not for a long time."

Sydney had been very quiet. She had a look on her face that told me she was thinking hard. She makes the same face when our teacher Mr. Luther gives us a tough math problem. It's usually a good thing, as Sydney's pretty good in math.

"There's got to be some way we can prove to our parents that we're ready for a dog," she said.

Just then, Nathan and Natalie walked by with Calvin.

"Hey guys!" Nathan called. "Want to play with Calvin?"

As much as I wanted to play with the dog, I knew it would make me feel worse. I didn't have to worry about hurting Nathan's feelings, though. Before we could say anything, the dog pulled Nathan down the sidewalk.

"Looks like he wants to keep walking," Nathan called. "Maybe next time!"

"Walking a dog looks like so much fun," Gomez said.

Sydney jumped up with a big smile on her face.

"That's it!" she said.

"What's it?" I asked.

"I know how we can convince our parents to let us get dogs!"

Sydney was so proud of her idea. She stood up and threw her arms out wide.

"We'll start a dog walking business!"

CHAPTER 4

Pooper
Scoopers

I expected everyone to cheer and tell me what a great idea it was. Instead, Harley, Sidney, and Gomez just stared at me. After a few seconds, I put my arms back down.

"How will walking other people's dogs change our parents' minds? Won't it make us want dogs even more?" Sidney asked.

"You aren't getting it. It's the perfect plan!" I told them. "It will show our parents that we are ready. I once helped water Mr. Thom's flowers while he was out of town. My mom said she was proud of how responsible I was. Helping take care of other people's dogs will show that we're responsible."

Sidney nodded his head. I could tell he was beginning to think it was a great idea. He said, "And we can use the money we make to help pay for all the things that dogs need, like food and vet visits."

"Exactly!" I said. I was happy that he was beginning to understand. Harley and Gomez still didn't look very excited, which seemed weird.

"What's wrong?" I asked them. "Don't you think it's a good idea?"

Harley frowned. "I think it's a great idea. I bet it will totally work."

"But it's not going to change *our* parents' minds," Gomez said.

I hadn't thought about that. Gomez's sister would still be allergic, and Harley's mom would still be a neat freak. So much for the perfect plan.

Harley shrugged her shoulders and said, "But it still sounds kind of fun. At least I could be around dogs."

Gomez nodded, "Good point. But I don't want to walk the big dogs!"

"No problem," Sidney said. "I'll walk all the big dogs! And when Sidney and I get our own dogs, you two can play with them whenever you want."

"Absolutely!" I agreed. "Since it was my idea, I'll be in charge. First thing we should do is figure out what we should call our business."

"How about Sidney's Dog Walking Company?" Sidney suggested.

"Oh! I like that!" I said.

"I meant Sidney with an 'i,'" he said to clarify.

I didn't like that as much.

"What about Goofy Gomez's Dog Walking Business?" Sidney asked, making a face at Gomez.

Gomez stuck out his tongue and replied, "No, I like Snotty Sidney's Dog Walkers."

"I'm serious you guys," I said. I was beginning to get mad at the boys for not taking my idea seriously. "We have so much to do! First, we need a good name for our business. Then, Harley and I can make flyers, and you guys can hang them up around town. We'll also have to figure out how much to charge and when we can walk the dogs."

"That sounds like a whole lot of work," Sidney said.

"It is, so you'd better stop fooling around and listen to me," I told him.

"Wait! I've got the perfect name," Gomez said excitedly. "How about Pooper Scoopers?"

Gomez and Sidney both burst out laughing. I was so frustrated.

"Gross," I said. Sometimes boys can be so annoying.

"We could get T-shirts that say 'Need a Pooper Scooper? Call us!'" Sidney said. He was laughing so hard he had tears in his eyes.

"Yeah!" Gomez replied. "And we could get matching hats with 'PS' on them for Pooper Scoopers!"

Why did boys think that kind of stuff was so funny? I crossed my arms and gave them a mean look. They were too busy laughing to notice that I was mad. Even Harley was laughing a little bit.

"If you can't be serious about this, then I'll think of a name on my own. It was my idea, anyway. Once Harley and I make the flyers, you two can hang them up."

Harley and I started to walk away. The boys were still laughing. I had had it! I turned around and snapped, "And I'm glad you think scooping poop is so funny since that will be your job!"

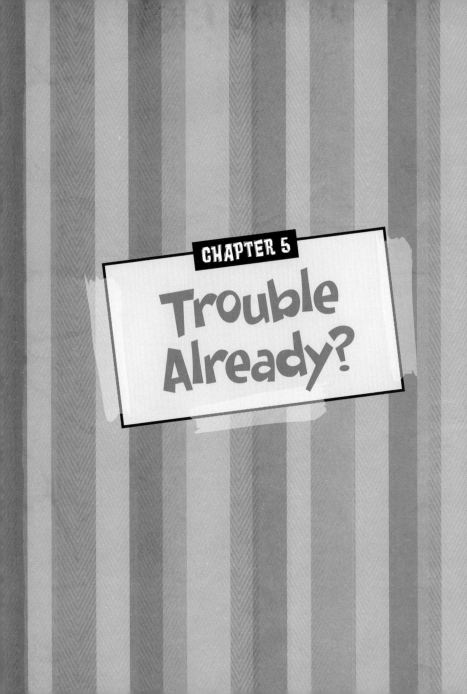

CHAPTER 5

Trouble Already?

At first I didn't understand Sydney's idea. When I thought about it some more, it began to make sense. My mom thought it was a great idea. She said something about it getting this whole dog thing out of my system. I'm not sure what that meant, but I'm glad she was happy about it.

Sydney's parents were happy about it, too. Her mom helped her on the computer. They made some great flyers to hang around the neighborhood. It had a bunch of pictures of dogs. In the middle it said, "Happy Tails — we walk all types of dogs."

Happy Tails wasn't as funny as Pooper Scoopers, but I didn't really care. Sydney had printed the flyers on bright paper. She said it would get people's attention. I had to admit, they looked really professional.

"I hope these flyers work," I said to Gomez.

"Me too," he replied.

Gomez and I had to cut little strips with Sydney's phone number at the bottom of each flyer. It took forever! Sydney wanted us to hang up flyers all over town. We had already hung them up at ten different places and had been walking for over an hour. We were both getting tired, so we sat down on the curb.

"I can't wait to start walking dogs," Gomez said.

"I know," I agreed. "Dogs are so much fun. We can play with them and take care of them."

It was then that I noticed Gomez had a weird look on his face.

"What's wrong?" I asked.

Gomez frowned. "Sydney's right. This dog walking business is a lot of work, and we haven't even walked one dog! Do you think she meant it when she said we'd have to pick up all the poop? I don't mind picking up some of it, but it should be fair. We can't do it all."

I nodded my head. "She has been pretty bossy about this whole thing. I bet she and Harley are watching TV while we're out here doing all the work. Maybe we should start our own dog walking business?"

"Maybe." Gomez didn't look too sure. "It was Sydney's idea, though."

"You're right." I sighed. "Plus, I don't have the energy to start over."

Just then, Sydney and Harley walked up. Sydney did not look happy. In fact, she looked a little scary.

"Do you guys need help hanging up flyers?" she snapped.

"Uh, sure," I replied and handed her some flyers. She snatched them out of my hand and walked toward the next store.

"What's with her?" I asked Harley.

"Her mom found out that you and Gomez were doing all the work. She made her come out and help," Harley said. "Sydney wasn't too happy about it."

Sydney could be so dramatic! So far her idea had lead to arguing and a lot of work.

But if I wanted to get my dog, we'd have to make this work. We've worked together before, and we've never had trouble.

I caught up with Sydney. She was having trouble with the tape, so I put out my hand to help her.

"Thanks," she grumbled and handed me the tape. "My mom says if we are all going to be a part of the business, we all have to help."

"I agree," I said. "With all of us helping, it will make things easier, right?"

Sydney smiled a little bit. "I guess I hadn't thought of it that way. I just really want this to work."

"So do we," I said. "Speaking of being a team — you're not really going to make me and Gomez pick up all the dog poop, are you?"

She rolled her eyes. "Of course not! Can't you two take a joke? Come on, we've got a lot more signs to hang up. If we split up, we'll get it done quicker."

She was still being bossy, but at least she wasn't so angry.

CHAPTER 6

No Dogs Means No Business

"Has anyone called yet?" Harley asked. The two of us were sitting on my front porch waiting for the phone to ring.

I turned the phone on to make sure it was working. It was, which made me feel even worse.

"Not yet," I told her.

It had been three days, and no one had called us about Happy Tails. Not one phone call. I was starting to worry.

Gomez and Sidney rode up on their bikes, looking even more despressed than me and Harley.

"Any luck?" I asked.

"Nope," Sidney said glumly.

"We saw two people walking their dogs, but neither wanted our help. They said they liked the exercise," Gomez said. "So much for being helpful."

Sidney got off his bike and sat on the steps. "We're never going to get dogs."

I looked at my three friends sitting sadly on the porch. I felt awful. This whole dog walking business had been my idea. We had worked so hard to make the flyers and hang them up.

Plus, I really wanted my little dog. I was not going to give up! I couldn't give up! I marched off toward my neighbor Mrs. West's house.

"Where are you going?" Harley called.

"To get us a client!" I yelled over my shoulder. I have never been more determined about anything in my life — not even playing *Galaxy Conquest*!

The three of them jumped up and followed me. My heart was pounding as I knocked on Mrs. West's front door. I had no idea what I was going to say, but I felt very determined.

Mrs. West looked surprised to see us when she answered the door.

"Well, hello kids!" she said. "What brings you by? Did Buster cause trouble again?"

Buster was Mrs. West's bulldog. He was always getting out of her yard and digging holes around the neighborhood.

"No, but we wanted to talk to you about Buster." I took a deep breath and kept going. "We've started a new business walking dogs and were wondering if you'd like us to walk Buster. He seems to really like walking around the neighborhood. I thought he might like it even more if he did it with us."

At first Mrs. West didn't say anything. I took another deep breath and rubbed my sweaty palms on my dress. This had to work or we were doomed.

"I have been kind of bad about walking him myself," Mrs. West said. "I guess he might like it if you got him out every once in a while."

As if he knew we were talking about him, Buster ran down the hallway and out the front door. Gomez didn't see him coming. Buster knocked him right over. Poor Gomez.

"Buster! Get back here!" Mrs. West called.

"I'll get him," Sidney said. In a flash, he was holding Buster by the collar.

"Oh, thank you!" Mrs. West smiled. "I think having you walk Buster would be wonderful! Do you think you could start today?"

We all nodded excitedly. As Mrs. West went to get Buster's leash, we jumped up and down and tried not to scream.

"Happy Tails is officially in business!" I said.

CHAPTER 7

A Very Pampered Princess

After we got Buster, our business really took off. Gomez and I were excited as we went to walk our newest dog named Princess. Her owner, Ms. Meyers, had twisted her ankle. She couldn't walk Princess for a few weeks.

Princess was the type of dog Sydney wanted. She looked like a white ball of fluff and would look perfect in one of those puppy purse things. Princess lived right next door to Sydney.

At first I didn't know why Sydney would choose to walk Buster with Harley instead of Princess. I soon found out why.

"Princess has very delicate feet. Make sure she walks half the time on the sidewalk and half the time on the grass," Ms. Myers told us. She had been giving us directions on how to walk Princess for over ten minutes. Who knew walking a little dog could be so complicated?

The whole time Ms. Myers was talking, Princess was barking and running around in circles. When I tried to pet her, she growled and showed me her teeth.

Ms. Myers went on, "Make sure you stay away from the Laurence's house.

They have a big dog that scares my little Princess."

With all the barking and growling Princess was doing, I found it hard to believe she was scared of anything!

"Halfway through the walk, let Princess stop and rest and give her a treat. Don't let her walk too far, or she'll get overtired and grumpy," Ms. Myers said. I made sure not to look at Gomez. I knew if I did, I would start laughing. This was ridiculous!

Finally, Ms. Myers put a sweater on Princess and handed me her leash. The dog looked so silly in that sweater! If she weren't so mean, I'd almost feel sorry for her.

"Oh! One more thing," Ms. Myers called as we walked out the door. "Take this umbrella."

I looked up at the sky. I didn't see a single cloud.

"It doesn't look like rain," I said, trying to be nice.

"It's for the sun, silly. And in case you forget, I put all the instructions on these cards." Ms. Myers handed Gomez a pile of index cards with writing on both sides.

"Uh, thanks," he said as he took the cards, trying not to laugh.

Gomez and I didn't say a word until we got to the end of the street and turned the corner. Then we both burst out laughing.

"That was crazy!" Gomez said. "I bet babysitting a baby would be easier!"

"I bet a baby wouldn't try to bite us, either!" I replied.

When we were about halfway through the walk, I stopped to give Princess her doggie treat.

"Hey! She hasn't barked the whole walk," Gomez said.

"You're right. That's strange," I said. I bent down and pet Princess on the top of her little head. She stood up on her back two legs like she wanted me to keep petting her. When I did, she jumped up to lick my face. Then she twirled around like a ballerina.

"Is this the same dog?" I asked. I didn't know why, but Princess seemed much calmer when she wasn't around Ms. Myers and all her crazy rules!

We were about to keep walking when I saw Mrs. Frank coming toward us. She was walking her two dogs, Missy and Max. She was still dressed in her work clothes. She looked to be in a rush.

"Hello, Mrs. Frank," Gomez and I said.

"Hello there, boys," she replied. "Is that Princess you're walking? I heard Patty Myers had hurt her ankle."

"It is," Gomez told her. "We started a dog walking business with Sydney and Harley. It's called Happy Tails."

"Really?" Mrs. Frank's eyes grew wide. "That's great! Ever since my kids went off to college, Missy and Max have not been getting walked enough. We try to get them out, but Mr. Frank and I have been so busy with work. Can I hire you?"

"You bet!" I said.

We worked out a schedule with Mrs. Frank and hurried to get Princess home on time. Gomez and I were so excited. Happy Tails was going better than we'd hoped!

CHAPTER 8

Rain or
Shine —
UGH!

Happy Tails was going great. We had a lot of dogs to walk and had been saving a bunch of money. It was adding up quickly. However, we spent so much time walking dogs that we didn't have much time for anything else.

I was glad when I woke up on Saturday and it was raining. I was supposed to walk Mrs. Lee's poodle with Gomez, but I really didn't feel like it. I was happy about the bad weather. It was a good excuse not to walk any dogs.

Plus, my friend Aubrey had invited me over. I was heading out the door when I heard my mom.

"Heading over to Mrs. Lee's?" she called from the kitchen. "I am so proud of you, Sydney, for taking this dog walking business seriously."

"Thanks, Mom, but I'm not walking Fifi today. It's raining."

My mom looked out the window.

"It's just drizzling," she said. "Besides, dogs need to be walked even in bad weather. It's part of taking care of them."

I felt my face get hot. Tears were stinging my eyes. I liked that my mom said she was proud, but I really didn't want to walk a dog today. I just wanted one day to play with my friend and not be responsible.

"But it's raining!" I whined. I was trying hard not cry.

"This is what I meant when I said dogs were a lot of work," my mom said, handing me an umbrella. "They need to be taken out in all kinds of weather."

"Even snow?" I asked. I hadn't thought about that. Some days it got so cold my mom would drive me to school so we wouldn't have to wait at the bus stop. Now I was going to have to walk a dog in that weather?

"Yep," my mom said. "You'd better get going. You don't want to be late."

I opened the umbrella and headed over to Mrs. Lee's. Gomez was waiting out front for me. He had his hood up and his head down. He looked as miserable as I felt.

Mrs. Lee was so happy to see us. "Thank you both! Fifi really looks forward to these walks! I don't get around like I used to. Just a short one today will be fine in this rain."

Fifi did seem happy to see us, and Mrs. Lee was so grateful. I knew we had done the right thing, so why didn't I feel happier?

CHAPTER 9

How to Impress Older Kids

"Hurry up!" I said, "They're going to start playing soon."

"I'm going as fast as I can," Gomez replied. I didn't believe him.

Gomez's older brother Lucas and his friends played football most days after school. I loved football, and I liked watching them play. Secretly, I was hoping they would let me play sometime. Gomez did not like playing football (or his brother Lucas), but he was a good friend so he went with me.

We were busy planting flowers in Mr.
Thom's yard while Sydney and Harley
walked the dogs. Mr. Thom wasn't one
of our dog walking clients. He lived next
door to Pancake, a crazy mutt we walked
sometimes. Pancake had gotten away from
me and Gomez when we were walking
him. He went straight for Mr. Thom's
flower beds. He'd dug up half the flowers
before we could stop him!

We talked about it with our parents. They explained that these things can happen when you have a business. They said it was up to us to make things right with Mr. Thom.

Sydney, Harley, Gomez, and I had a company meeting. We decided to use some of the money we'd made to buy flowers to replace the ones Pancake had dug up. Mr. Thom was happy with our solution.

I felt good about doing the right thing. I was annoyed, though, that we had to use so much of the money we had earned.

"Looks good, boys," Mr. Thom said when we'd finished. "Thank you for your hard work."

"Thank you, Mr. Thom," Gomez said.

"Sorry again about the flowers. We'll keep a better eye on Pancake," I told him.

We turned and ran for Gomez's house. When we got there, Lucas and his friends were just getting started.

Lucas saw us coming and asked, "Wat is wrong with you? Why are you so out of breath and covered in dirt?"

I wiped my hands on my jeans and said, "We were planting flowers."

"Flowers? I thought you guys were walking dogs?" Lucas asked.

"It's a long story," I said. Lucas's friends were looking at us.

Lucas turned to his friends and said, "These two goofballs spend all their time walking other people's dogs. Isn't that crazy?"

Lucas's friend Pete shrugged his shoulders and asked, "Do you get paid?"

Gomez replied, "Yes! A lot!"

"I wouldn't say a lot . . ." I started, but Gomez kept right on talking.

"We make so much money!" he said. "And it is so easy! All we do is walk a few dogs around the block. It's the best job in the world!"

Lucas's friends seemed impressed. They usually tease us. It was nice to have them be nice to us for a change. One of them even asked if we needed any help.

"We're good for now, but we'll keep you in mind," Gomez said.

He seemed to be really enjoying the attention. I have to admit, planting flowers was a pain, but it did feel good to impress a bunch of 13-year-olds!

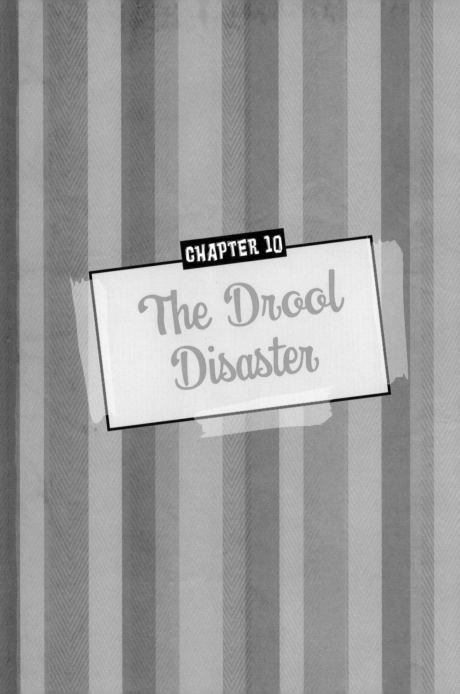

CHAPTER 10

The Drool Disaster

"Why are you so dressed up?" Sidney asked when I answered the door.

I was wearing a brand-new outfit: zebra print leggings under a black skirt and a pink top with sequins. It was totally adorable. "We're going out for dinner tonight to celebrate my dad's birthday."

"Oh," he replied. "So you are going to wear that to walk Louie?"

"Yes. That's why I have it on," I said.

"Seems weird, but okay. Let's go," he said as we started toward the Laurence's house to get Louie.

I was glad I had on a cute outfit to cheer me up, because I was not happy to be walking another dog. I had been thinking about the dog walking business a lot lately. I was sort of sick of walking dogs. They were all nice dogs, and it felt good to be helping people and making money. But I was tired of it taking up all my time. Having a business was a lot of work.

I thought about saying something to Sidney, but before I could, we were at the Laurence's.

Mrs. Laurence was one of my favorite neighbors. She was always in a good mood. She looked frustrated, though, as she answered the door. Her dog, Louie, was barking up a storm and trying to get out. Louie was a black and tan coonhound and one of the biggest dogs in the neighborhood.

"Louie! Settle down!" she said to the dog. Then she turned to us. "Come on in, guys. Thanks so much for doing this."

I looked over at Sidney. I wasn't too sure about walking this dog. I was surprised to see that Sidney had a huge smile on his face. He looked super excited.

"Your dog is amazing!" Sidney said.

Mrs. Laurence put a leash on Louie and handed it to Sidney. "He can be quite a handful. If he's too much for you, please feel free to bring him back."

"He's awesome!" Sidney said. "This is exactly the kind of dog I want to get!"

"You can have him," Mrs. Laurence said with a smile.

"Really?" Sidney's eyes got big.

"Unfortunately, no," Mrs. Laurence laughed. "My husband loves this big crazy dog."

"You don't?" I asked. I was starting to think that maybe I didn't want a dog. It was sort of nice to find another person who felt the same way.

"Dogs are a lot of work," she said. "When we first got Louie he was into everything! He would eat socks, toys, and video games."

"Video games?" Sidney and I said at the same time. I would be so upset if a dog ate my copy of *Galaxy Conquest* or *Galaxy Conquest 2!*

I knew Sidney loved *Galaxy Conquest* as much as I did. Surely he wouldn't want a dog now that he knew it might eat his games. This would be the perfect time to talk to him about quitting the business.

"Isn't Louie awesome?" he said as we walked down the driveway. "I want a dog just like him!"

"But what about your video games?"
I asked.

"I'll just have to put them where he
can't get them," Sidney said. "My mom
is always bugging me to pick up my stuff
anyway."

I didn't know what to do. Happy Tails
had been my idea. Sidney seemed more
excited than ever to get a dog, but I
wanted out.

Just then Louie stopped suddenly on
the sidewalk. I got closer to see what was
wrong. I noticed that he had a long strand
of thick drool dripping from his mouth. I
was about to say how gross it looked when
Louie shook his whole body.

Drool went flying everywhere! I was standing so close I couldn't get out of the way in time. When he stopped shaking, I opened my eyes. There was drool all over my brand-new outfit!

That was the last straw. I knew for sure that I wanted out of this business! No more Happy Tails for this girl!

"And then slobber flew everywhere!" I could barely finish telling Gomez the story about Louie slobbering on Sydney without cracking up. Gomez was laughing so hard I thought he was going to pee his pants.

I noticed Sydney was standing with her arms crossed. She looked mad, so I tried to stop laughing. Sydney had been in a bad mood all day. She wasn't talking much, either. That was very strange for her (and quiet for us). I thought it might be about Louie ruining her clothes, but that had been days ago.

Harley, Gomez, Sydney, and I were meeting to plan our dog walking for the week. When we started doing this, it was fun planning the walks. We all wanted to walk our favorite dogs. Now we weren't so excited about it.

"I have basketball practice starting next week. I can't walk any dogs on Tuesday or Thursday after school or on Saturday morning," I told them. I couldn't wait for basketball to start! It was my favorite sport by far.

"Me too," Gomez said. Even though Gomez wasn't very tall, he was fast. We made a great team.

"I have soccer on Monday, Wednesday, and Saturday afternoons," Harley said. She was a great soccer player. She played on a team that traveled all over for games, which was pretty cool.

"I've got play practice three nights next week, too," Sydney said. She'd had so much fun in our school play that she joined a local theater group. I'll probably never do another play again, but Sydney was a good actress. I think it's because she is so dramatic.

I looked at the list of dogs we needed to walk. It was a big list, and we were all really busy.

"How are we going to get this all done?" I asked. "I can't miss basketball."

"Me neither," said Gomez.

"Well I can't miss play practice!" Sydney said, crossing her arms again.

"There's no way I can miss soccer," Harley said.

I was so frustrated! Nobody was willing to give up anything, but we had all these dogs to walk.

* * *

Later that night I told my mom about our problem.

"That's a tough one," she said. "You've taken on a lot of responsibility. Now it sounds like you've got some tough choices to make."

"Choices?" I asked. "What do you mean?"

"Well, you've made a commitment to your friends and your clients. You've also made a commitment to your basketball team. It sounds like you can't honor both of them at the same time."

"But I really want a dog! I thought this would show you that I could take care of one." I was trying not to cry, but I felt tears in my eyes. I didn't want to seem like a baby, but sometimes even boys have to cry.

"Oh honey," my mom said. "Watching you start this business has made me so proud. I'm glad, though, that it's has shown you how much work goes in to taking care of an animal."

"It sure has," I mumbled.

"And the commitment of having a pet doesn't go away when you get busy with other things," she said.

I hadn't thought of that before.

"Maybe you're right. Maybe I'm not ready for a dog," I said softly.

"Maybe not yet, but you're close," my mom said. "When the time is right, you are going to be a great dog owner."

I lifted my head up. "You mean I can get a dog one day?"

"You've shown me that you can be very responsible," she said. "When we are both ready, we can definitely get a dog."

I was so happy! "Can we get a big dog like Louie?" I asked.

My mom shook her head. "That sounds like a discussion for another time!"

CHAPTER 12

The Perfect Plan

I was done with Happy Tails. The only problem was how to tell the others. I thought Sidney felt the same way until we walked Louie. I knew he still really wanted a dog.

I had decided I didn't want a dog anymore. Instead I wanted a kitten. Kittens don't need to be walked, and I could still carry it around in a purse. My mom loves cats. When I asked her about getting a kitten, she said maybe. Everyone knows maybe is practically a yes.

We were meeting at Sidney's to try to figure out next week's walking schedule again. We had tried the day before, but everyone had gotten mad and gone home.

The whole way over to Sidney's I thought about how I could tell everyone I wanted out. I felt so bad. Happy Tails had been my idea, and now I was bailing.

As I walked up to Sidney's house, I saw Harley, Gomez, and Sidney standing on the porch. I took a deep breath and walked up.

Before I could say a word, Sidney said, "We all want to quit Happy Tails."

"What?" I asked. I was so confused. "I thought you all loved Happy Tails?"

"We all love the dogs," Harley said, "but we all have other things we'd rather do. I can't give up soccer, and I don't have time for both."

I turned toward Sidney and asked, "Don't you still want to get a dog?"

"That's the best part," he said. "My mom was so happy with how hard we worked she said that when we were both ready we could get a dog. I don't know exactly when, but at least I know we will."

"That's great!" I said. I was so relieved! This was working out perfectly. Then I realized that nobody looked as happy as I felt, which didn't make any sense. Clearly I was missing something.

"What's wrong? Why do you guys look sad? We all want out, right?"

"Sure," said Gomez, "but what about our customers? We can't just leave them."

I had been so worried about telling my friends that I hadn't thought about that part.

"Part of showing my mom that I'm responsible enough for a dog is finding a way to quit Happy Tails without upsetting all the neighbors," Sidney said.

We all sat quietly thinking. I had been the one to think up the dog walking business, but I was having trouble finding a way out.

"I wish we could just think of something quick," Gomez said. "Lucas and his friends are playing football today. Now that they think we're cool, I kind of like watching them play."

Suddenly Sidney smiled and said, "That's it!"

"What's it?" I asked, totally confused.

Sidney looked excited as he said, "Everyone go and get a dog and meet at Gomez's. I have the perfect plan!"

CHAPTER 13

The Plan in Action

My plan just had to work! All of us were ready to quit Happy Tails, and we needed to do it quickly.

Harley, Gomez, Sydney, and I each picked up one of our dog clients and met at the corner of Gomez's street. I could see that Lucas and his friends were out front getting ready to play football. I quickly went over the plan, and we began slowly walking toward them.

When we were about a house away, I started talking loudly. "I can't believe we have so many dogs to walk!"

"I know!" Gomez shouted loudly. Too loudly. Sydney nudged him, and he spoke more normally. "With all of these dogs, we're going to make so much money."

I noticed that a few of the guys were looking over at us. As we got closer we slowed down. I gave a small nod to Sydney. She said, "Who knew a dog walking business could be so much fun? I can't believe people pay us to walk and play with these adorable dogs!"

She bent down and started petting Princess. As soon as she did, Princess

began to twirl around on her back legs.
Sydney gave her a treat. Princess did a few
more tricks.

I knew Sydney was a good actress, but
I didn't realize she was that good. She
looked like she was having so much fun.
Watching her with Princess almost made
me want to keep Happy Tails!

Lucas and his friends walked over to where we were.

"Does she do any other tricks?" Jamel, one of Lucas's friends, asked.

"Oh sure," Sydney said. Princess rolled over and played dead. She seemed to be enjoying the attention.

Two of Lucas's friends began chasing Buster. A couple others were laughing as they watched Pancake chase his tail around and around.

"Well, we'd better get going," I said. "We need to go get the money we make from playing with these dogs. It's really starting to add up!"

My acting was not as good as Sydney's, but I certainly got their attention.

"You get paid to play with these dogs?" another friend named Pete asked.

"Yep," said Harley. "We've got a dog walking business called Happy Tails. It's super fun."

"We should start a business like that!" said another boy. "How do you do it?"

"We already walk most of the dogs in the neighborhood," Sydney told them. "I don't know if you could get any other clients."

"Then we'll just work with you," Lucas said, crossing his arms over his chest.

"The business is technically ours, so you'd be working for us," I reminded him. "We'd be the bosses."

Lucas and his friends were a lot older and bigger than us. I was sort of nervous. I knew Lucas would never go for having his little brother be his boss.

"No way!" he said. "I want to be the boss!"

"Besides, since we're older, we'd probably do a better job," Pete said. "We could take over the business from you. Then we'd be the bosses. You guys would work for us."

"I don't know," Sydney spoke up. "Are you sure you want to work with a bunch of third graders? You could probably do it better by yourselves."

They all nodded in agreement. I could tell they all liked the idea of running a dog walking business.

"We sure could!" Lucas said. "Why don't you let us take over Happy Tails?"

I smiled at Sydney, Harley, and Gomez. My planned had worked!

CHAPTER 14

Ready for a Doggie Break

"Sidney, you are a genius," I said as we walked down the street.

We had gone to see all of our dog walking clients. We told them that Lucas and his friends were going to be taking over. We let them know that not much would change other than the name of the business. They had changed it to Super Awesome Dog Walkers.

"I can't believe Lucas and his friends fell for that!" Sidney said with a laugh.

"I know," Gomez said. "It was perfect! Are you sure you still want a big dog after all the work we just did?"

Sidney laughed, "Yes! The bigger the better. I put all the money I made from Happy Tails in the bank for when my mom is ready."

"Is it hard for you to wait?" I asked.

"Not really," he replied. "After all that dog walking, I'm ready for a break!"

I felt the same way. The dogs were so cute, but I was tired of so much walking and not having any free time.

My mom and dad had been so proud of me. Plus, I was saving my dog walking money. I had heard they were making a *Galaxy Conquest 3*, and I wanted to get it the day it came out.

We were just about to my house when we saw Nathan and his dog Calvin walking up the street.

"What's up, Nathan?" I asked.

"Not much," Nathan said. Then he let out a big yawn. "I'm just sort of tired. Calvin was afraid of the thunderstorm last night. He kept me up all night."

We all stopped to play with Calvin. He didn't seem half as tired as Nathan!

Nathan let out another really big yawn. "I'd really like to go home and rest, but my mom said I have to walk Calvin. Do you guys want to walk him for me?" he asked.

We all looked at each other for minute.

"Not today," Sidney said. "Maybe another time."

"Okay," Nathan said and kept walking. "Thanks anyway."

As Nathan walked, away we all laughed. We knew it would be a while before any of us would want to walk another dog!

WHAT WOULD BE YOUR IDEAL PET?

Sydney: Something cute and fluffy that I could dress up and carry in my purse.

Sidney: A big dog. A really, really, really big dog. A dog like Louie.

WHAT WOULD BE YOUR NIGHTMARE PET?

Sydney: A snake. Gross.

Sidney: A talking bird. My grandma had one. At first it was fun, but after a while it was annoying.

WHAT DID YOU LIKE ABOUT HAPPY TAILS?

Sydney: Spending more time with my friends.

Sidney: Playing with the dogs.

WHAT DIDN'T YOU LIKE ABOUT HAPPY TAILS?

Sydney: All the poop!

Sidney: I agree! Poop is funny but really gross.

WOULD YOU DO IT AGAIN?

Sydney: Yes! I learned a lot!

Sidney: Of course! It was hard but super awesome.

IF YOU WERE AN ANIMAL, WHAT WOULD YOU BE?

Sydney: A horse.

Sidney: A skunk.

ABOUT THE AUTHOR

Raised in the Chicago suburb of Hoffman Estates, Michele Jakubowski has the teachers in her life to thank for her love of reading and writing. While writing has always been a passion for Michele, she believes it is the books she has read throughout the years, and the teachers who assigned them, that have made her the storyteller she is today. Michele lives in Powell, Ohio, with her husband, John, and their children, Jack and Mia.

ABOUT THE ILLUSTRATOR

Luisa Montalto followed a curved path to becoming an illustrator. She was first a dancer, then earned her doctorate degree in cinematography. She credits these experiences with giving her the energy and will to try harder. Finally, she went on to work with an independent comics magazine before becoming a professional illustrator in 2003.